Il Goatino

Written by Roggen Zyrro

Illustrated by Ruth Shields

Printed by
The Covington Group
Kansas City, MO

Il Goatino

To KIARA & KADIAN

[signature]

a.k.a. Roggen Zyrros

Il Goatino – the smiling bah-bah,

the bearded frisky-boy –

stuck his horns in a fat stack of sacks.

The goat got oats!

It's not every beast who can crunch his lunch!

And with a mouthful to munch,

his crunch packed a punch!

Il Goatino had quick, shifty moves and a head as hard as a stone.

Whenever he jumped on his dad's broad back,

his hooves had room to roam.

But he'd always get thrown, run off alone and chase himself home.

The rings around Il Goatino's eyes were cocoa-colored swirls.
His coat looked like cookie-dough ice cream that was painted
with stripes and curls.

He was cute to the girls.
He was kind to the squirrels.
His tail swatted bugs with a twirl.

Il Goatino was a young pygmy kid who
made sounds like a squeaky-toy sheep.

Birds called back with chirps and peeps,
cheeps and tweets.
(It wasn't even trick or treat!)

The rooster crowed over the honks of the geese,
and even a screech owl screeched.

But the hounds stayed quietly asleep; they'd had too much to eat.

Children came by to spend time with him.

They smiled and whispered how much they all loved him.

Il Goatino nuzzled his muzzle in a feed-box nailed to the fence.

He liked to be petted, but not to be hugged,

and picking him up made him tense.

He ate some alfalfa and danced.

Il Goatino's favorite days were the holidays he spent inside.

He loved . . .

Christmas!

He loved . . .

Thanksgiving!

And he loved . . .

Birthdays! . . .

which are the same as holidays to a goat!

But most of all, Il Goatino loved **Mother's Day!**

And he was everyone's favorite son.

Il Goatino bit an oak and gave it a lick for a taste.

The bark was hard and bitter like smoke, so he kicked some acorns away.

The tree didn't care and it stayed there, while the goat took a walk in a circle.

He had a seat. He chewed his feet. He wanted to be in a huddle.

Il Goatino wobbled and yawned and leaned against the tree.

A feather landed on his nose, another on his teeth.

The one in his mouth was nasty,

so he shook and coughed and sneezed.

Il Goatino widened his eyes and slowly peeked up at the leaves.

What did the little goat see?

Every branch held 50 crows, and every crow was black as coal –

except those that were bluish and purple.

A thick stick splashed in a puddle.

Il Goatino was all atremble!

(Sheep say *baah* and *behh* and *baah*.

And goats go *mehh* and *maah* and *maah*.

Il Goatino never said *mehh*. He only said *maah*.

And when he got scared, he went *mah-mah-maah!*)

Il Goatino sprang from the shade in a half-step, stuttered stumble.

He scrambled to the herd on the double, where he found his uncle and mumbled.

The old goat was chewing and grumbled.

Il Goatino trotted off with a shuffle, a snuffle, a tumble.

Il Goatino felt the wind and turned his face to the sky.

A drifting rainbow linked the clouds and pulled the bundle by.

The fluffy blobs of lumpy foam bobbed low enough to bite.

Il Goatino went on the hunt and leaped with all his might.

Zigging and zooming,
　the buckling was vrooming.

He was panting and puffing,
　and yes he was roughing.

He was snapping and yapping,
　and yipping and yakking.

And just when he had one ready for trapping! . . .
　the fence made him stop – which wasn't right, or very nice.

The clouds were floating out of sight!
And Il Goatino was penned in tight! . . .
squinting at the light,
　till the last speck of white was gone.

He said a few *maahs* and moved on –
　through the shadows of the setting sun.

Il Goatino jogged back to the goat-shack and had a snack.

He wrecked his bed with jumping jacks, hoof-smacks and sneak attacks.

He was too worked up to be sleepy,
  but his day of adventure was ending.

The moon was already rising.
  And the goats outside were gathering to the ringing of the evening bell.

Il Goatino bounced up and down.
  He jumped over and over and ran all around.

There was dust!

There was clatter!

No matter!

Il Goatino kissed his mother,

head-butted his brother

and pounced on a board by the barn.

He wanted to play a little longer –

to stay awake and have fun on the farm.

But soon he was tired,

and his mother was beside him,

making sure he would come to no harm.

She led Il Goatino to a freshly made bed

that was safe

and perfect

and warm.

Also available by Roggen Zyrro

Bunsta

For more information, visit
www.bunsta.com